THE BOY OF STEEL

REGAN

An Imprint of HarperCollins*Publishers*

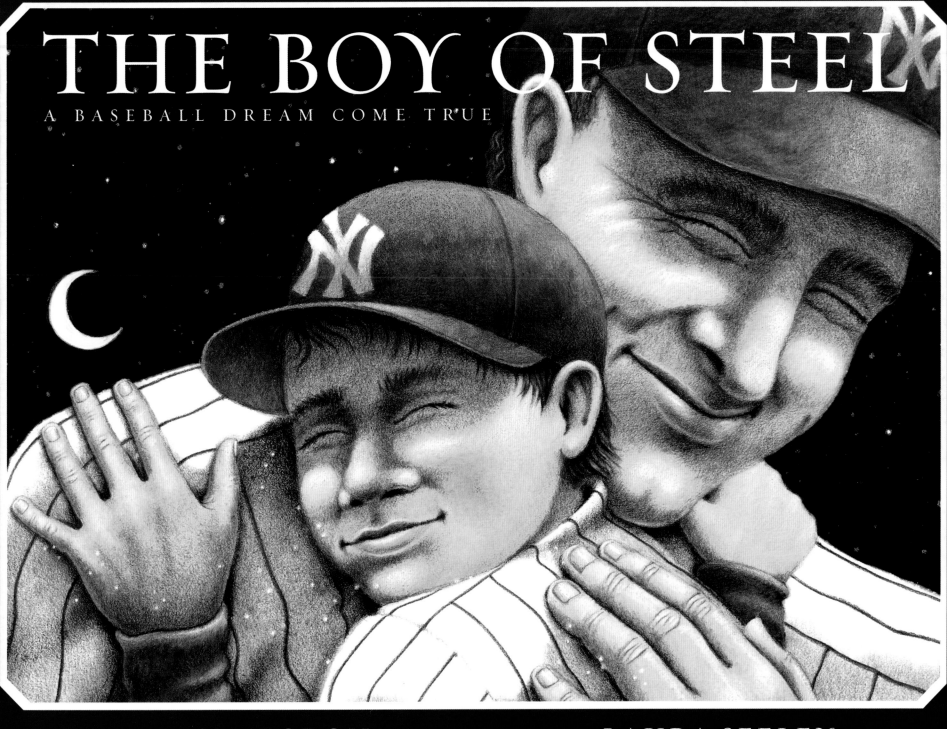

THE BOY OF STEEL

A BASEBALL DREAM COME TRUE

BY RAY NEGRON ILLUSTRATED BY LAURA SEELEY

To George M. Steinbrenner III

I am one of too many to count who the Boss has saved. He found me in the streets of New York at the age of sixteen and gave me direction. Thirty years later I proudly call him my friend and, of course, THE BOSS!

To Adele Smithers—a true friend

To millions, you will always be the mother of recovery.

And finally, to Michael Steele Wilkins— the real Boy of Steel

Your spirit will live forever.

FOREWORD

There's no greater bond known to mankind than the one between parent and child. The love is eternal, transcending all the physical limitations of this world. Whether your child is big or small, gifted or challenged, healthy or sick, the nurturing instinct is hard-wired into our souls. We appreciate everything about out children as they grow: their smiles, their laughter, even the air they breathe.

Children keep us young. Through them, we rediscover the pleasures of our own youth, whether it's riding on a merry-go-round while eating cotton candy or going to a major league baseball game for the first time. Although kids see their parents as the guiding light, in reality it's our children who open our eyes to the true meaning of life. Take a look at your sleeping son or daughter and you'll know why you were put on this earth.

Sometimes it takes pain to measure love. *The Boy of Steel* is a story about a little boy's fight with cancer, but it is also a reminder about loving what we have right now.

Every time we, as parents, read the passages in this book, we take a moment to count our blessings, both as husband and wife and as father and mother. *The Boy of Steel* lives forever. He inspires all of us.

—KELLY RIPA AND MARK CONSUELOS

"Yankees win! Thuuuhhhhhhh Yankees win!!!"

Michael Steel watched the baseball highlights on the television mounted on the wall across from him in the children's cancer ward in the hospital. Michael's parents sat alongside his bed and watched with him.

"I sure wish I could have been there last night," said Michael.

"We'll go when you get better. I promise," said his father.

"The Yankees are the best, and so are you, Dad!" Michael raised a clenched fist to the air, as the IV tube swung from his left arm.

Then Michael's mother said, "We have a surprise for you." Mrs. Steel gestured toward the door of the hospital room. "He's here right now."

Michael quickly turned his head, but the curtain surrounding his bed blocked his view. Mrs. Steel pushed it back, revealing . . .

. . . New York Yankees second baseman, Robinson Cano. Michael's eyes widened.

"Robinson Cano? I can't believe it! Robinson Cano is actually here! In my room!"

The second baseman approached Michael and extended his right hand. "That's right, Michael. I'm here to help you get well. But please, just call me Robbie."

Michael eagerly shook Robbie's large hand.

Robbie told Michael about Yankee greats of the past. He told Michael funny stories about current players.

Michael pointed to Robbie's short haircut and said, "Hey, you're almost bald like me!" Michael's hair had fallen out from the many chemotherapy sessions he had been through.

As Robbie left Michael's room, he turned to Michael and said, "I hope you can watch the game tonight. I'm going to try to hit a home run just for you. And I want you to try to hit one for me."

Later that night, Michael asked the nurse if he could stay up late and watch the Yankees play the Red Sox on TV.

With two outs in the bottom of the ninth inning, it was Robbie's turn to hit. As Robbie made his way to the batter's box, Michael closed his eyes and crossed his fingers.

The pitcher wound up and delivered a
fastball toward the plate. Robbie swung
from his heels and knocked the ball
deep into the right-field bleachers,
giving the Yankees a magical victory.
Michael's jubilant cheers echoed
throughout the corridor of the
children's hospital.

The next day, Mr. Steel walked into Michael's room.

"Did you see it, Dad? Robbie hit a home run for me, just like he said he would!"

"Yes, Michael, I saw it. That was great! Hey, would you like to go to Yankee Stadium tonight?" asked his father.

"But how . . . ?" asked Michael. "I haven't gotten better yet."

"Well, your doctors said it would be okay just this once. After all, how often will you get the chance to be Robinson Cano's personal batboy?"

Michael's face lit up like a Christmas tree.

"I can't believe it! It's like a dream!"

He scrambled from his bed and hugged his father.

That night, Robbie led Michael into the clubhouse of the famous Bronx Bombers. He stared at all the names on each locker. "Wow, that's Derek Jeter, and there's Hideki Matsui, and Bernie and A-Rod . . . and look! Ruben Sierra is bald, too!"

Michael stared at Robbie's clean pinstriped uniform, his shining spikes, and oiled glove—as well as a pile of wooden bats.

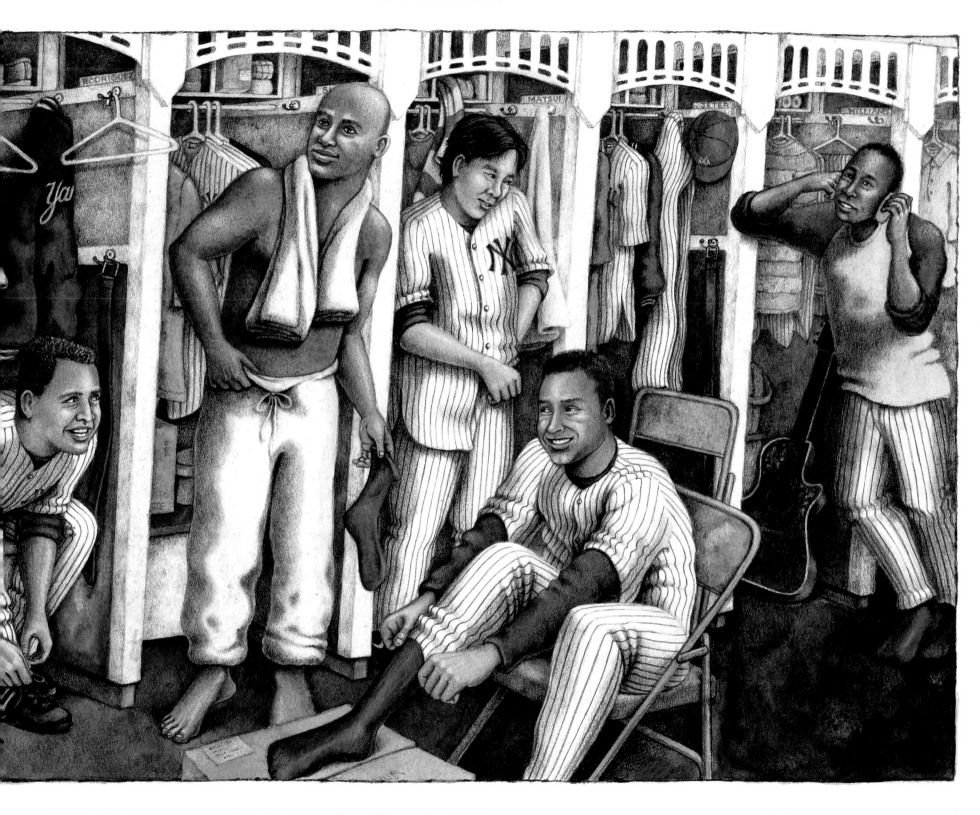

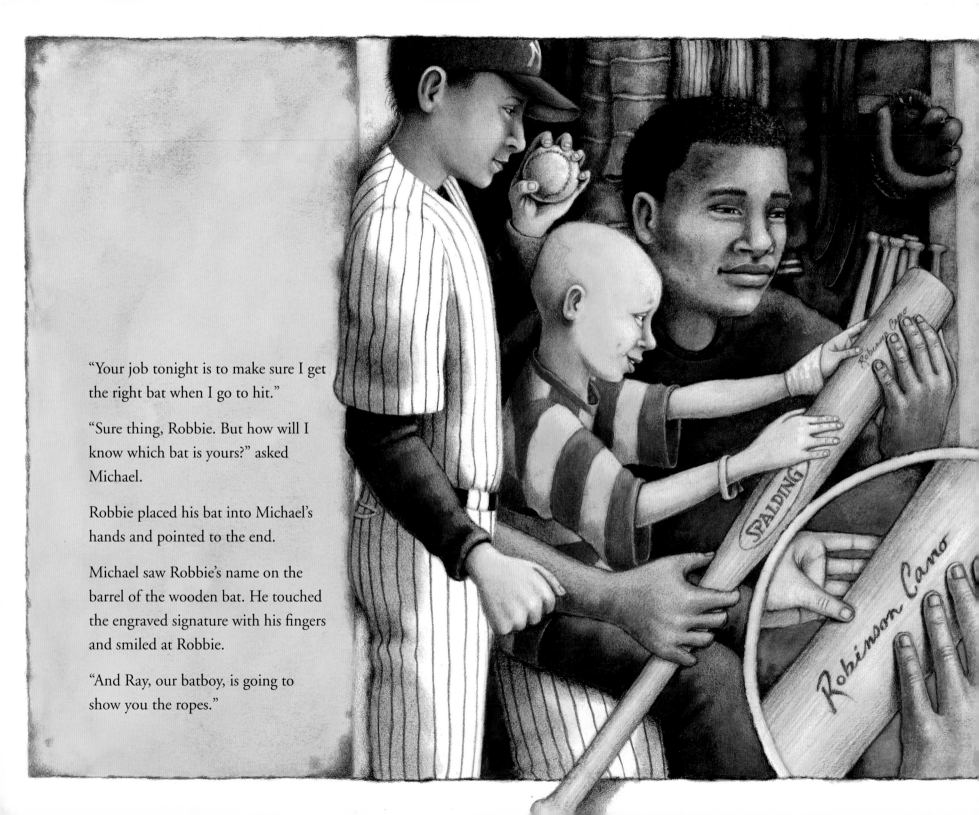

"Your job tonight is to make sure I get the right bat when I go to hit."

"Sure thing, Robbie. But how will I know which bat is yours?" asked Michael.

Robbie placed his bat into Michael's hands and pointed to the end.

Michael saw Robbie's name on the barrel of the wooden bat. He touched the engraved signature with his fingers and smiled at Robbie.

"And Ray, our batboy, is going to show you the ropes."

Ray got Michael outfitted with a Yankee uniform just like his, including a hat just like his, but with MICHAEL written on the underside of the bill in black marker.

Ray put a white towel in Michael's back pocket just like his.

As Ray showed Michael how to polish the players' helmets and spikes, a shadowy figure suddenly loomed over them.

It was the owner of the Yankees, George Steinbrenner! "I want to be able to see my reflection in that helmet, son."

"Y-y-yes, sir," Michael stammered. "Robbie told me you broke the rules to let me in the clubhouse. Thanks."

"You'll earn it, young man, you'll earn it," said Mr. Steinbrenner as he patted Michael on the top of his head, giving encouragement to the young batboy before leaving the room.

After finishing their clubhouse duties, Ray took Michael on a behind-the-scenes tour of Yankee Stadium. At the end of the corridor, past the batting cage, Ray took out a gold-colored key, opened a large padlock, and rolled up a squeaky steel shutter.

"What's in here?" asked Michael.

"It's just an old storage room. Only team members are allowed in here. You're an honorary batboy, so you're now an official member of the Yankees family. Do you know the Golden Rule of the Yankees?" Ray asked. "Once a Yankee, always a Yankee."

"Even if it's for just one game?" asked Michael.

Ray nodded. "You'll be a Yankee forever."

Michael sat down on a broken row of seats under a single lightbulb.

"Robbie told me that you've been sick for some time. Brain cancer, right?"

"It's called neuroblastoma. Just the name really scares me," said Michael.

"I understand," said Ray. "My mother had breast cancer, but it just went into remission. I was scared too." He thought for a second. "You know, there's another Yankee who wants to talk to you about that."

"But, I've already met all the players."

"But this is a special Yankee. You'll like him," said Ray.

"Okay," said Michael. "Where is he?"

"Just close your eyes and count backward from ten. When you reach one, open your eyes and you'll see him."

Michael looked concerned, but Ray quickly eased his mind. "Don't be afraid." Michael took a deep breath, then closed his eyes and began counting backward from ten.

2000
Yank's Win 1st
Subway Series
in 44 Years

10 9

When he reached *one,* he opened his eyes and found himself sitting in the Yankees dugout.

Michael rubbed his eyes and stared at a Yankee player giving a speech in front of a large silver microphone.

"This can't be," said a mesmerized Michael, as he climbed the steps of the dugout for a closer look. "This just can't be."

"Today, I consider myself . . ."

It was Yankee great Lou Gehrig. Lou stopped for a brief second and glanced toward Michael.

". . . the luckiest man on the face of the earth."

Booming over the public address system was Lou Gehrig's farewell speech. It was July 4, 1939. Michael listened intently as the Iron Horse spoke.

The fans erupted with cheers and tears as Lou
waved to the crowd. Michael followed Lou as he
quickly made his way into the runway leading to
the clubhouse.

Michael tiptoed toward the once-mighty slugger,
who now sat beside his locker, wiping away the
tears that rolled down his craggy face. Michael
handed his white towel to Lou.

"Thank you, son."

"My name is Michael Steel."

"I know. I've been waiting for you," Lou replied.

"For me? But why?" asked Michael.

Lou turned to him, "Because you, Michael, truly represent courage."

Lou removed Michael's hat, revealing a full head of thick brown hair.

"No matter what the score may be or what inning you may be in, a true Yankee battles to the end and never gives up. If you try hard enough, you can do anything. You have that same spirit, my little friend. You are a true Yankee."

Lou reached out and mussed Michael's hair.

Lou and Michael talked and talked, sharing stories of bravery, courage, and hope. Lou knew what Michael was going through, for Lou was suffering from ALS, a different, but also terrible disease.

During Michael's visit, he was introduced to Babe Ruth, Joe DiMaggio, Mickey Mantle, and Roger Maris. Each legendary player shared a word of encouragement to the young batboy. They knew the battle Michael faced, for they too had battled cancer.

"Before you go, I have something for you," said Lou. "Many of the Yankee greats have nicknames. Mine is the Iron Horse, DiMaggio's nickname is Joltin' Joe, and Babe's nickname is, well . . . Babe. But you, my friend, have the greatest nickname of all time. You are the Boy of Steel."

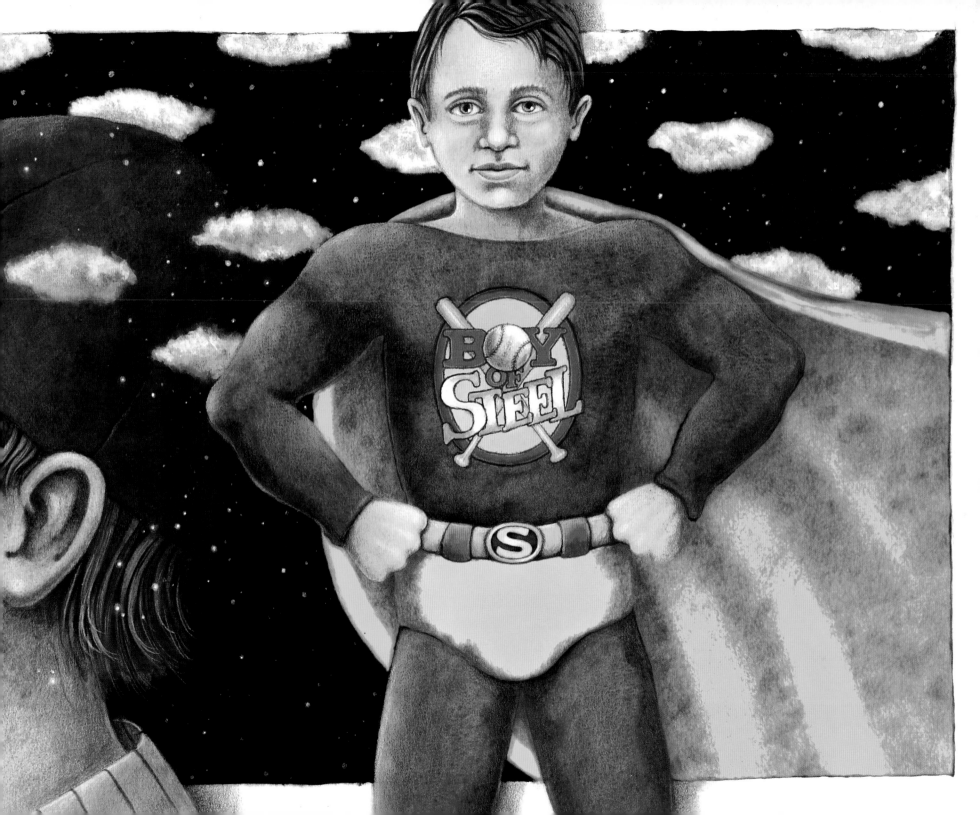

"With time, research, and a lot of love,
you can make it, Michael."

Michael thanked Lou
with a mighty hug.

Then Michael walked under the steel shutter. He sat on the broken stadium seat under the bare lightbulb and waved to Lou. Michael closed his eyes and counted backward from ten.

When Michael reached *one,* he opened one eye, not sure where he would end up this time. He found himself sitting among the current Yankees. The fans roared as Robinson Cano stepped to the plate.

Michael screamed to him, "Come on, Robbie! Hit another homer!"

With a count of three balls and one strike, Robbie
hit a fastball that climbed through the starry night
sky before landing in the upper deck.

Michael sprang from the dugout and ran as
fast as he could toward home plate.

He could feel the electricity of the cheering fans. But before he could reach Robbie's
bat, his vision became blurry and his lungs began to burn with every step.
Michael tumbled face-first into the grass . . .

. . . his hat flying off his head.

When Robbie rounded third base he saw Michael struggling to get to his feet. In an instant, his casual home run trot turned into a concerned, all-out sprint for home plate, and, more important, for Michael.

When he reached Michael, Robbie gently helped him up. He picked up Michael's baseball cap and gave it to him.

Michael began to place the cap back on his head. He checked for his name under the bill, to make sure it was his. Michael gasped at what he saw. There, instead of his first name, clear as day were the words BOY OF STEEL.

He remembered what Lou had said. "A true Yankee never gives up . . ."

An inner strength filled Michael's spirit. Michael took a deep breath, then picked up Robbie's bat and handed it to him, his arms shaking uncontrollably.

From the owner's box high above the playing field, The Boss applauded Michael's brave effort.

"Are you okay?" Robbie asked, frantically scooping Michael up off the grass.

"I'm better than okay, I'm great!" Michael said.

Robbie then placed Michael high upon his shoulder and carried him through a sea of pinstriped teammates. Over the ear-piercing sounds of fifty thousand cheering voices, Michael spoke into Robbie's ear and said, "You are my hero, Robbie."

"No, you are **my** hero, Michael," said Robbie. Michael's smile seemed brighter than the lights of Yankee Stadium, for it was the first time in Michael's life that his vision was totally clear and his lungs could finally breathe.

The Boy of Steel would forever be . . . . a New York Yankee.

LETTER FROM THE AUTHOR

The New York Yankees have a lot of tradition surrounding them. As if twenty-six World Series wins, all those great players whose numbers have been retired, the records set and broken, and the legions of fans all over the world weren't enough, there is one more Yankee tradition I want to mention. It all started with Babe Ruth, the great Sultan of Swat, who genuinely loved kids. Although the story of him promising to hit a homer for a sick kid in the hospital didn't quite happen in such a storybook way, it was based on a real incident. The Babe began a long Yankee tradition of visiting sick children in hospitals—kids who had incurable diseases, kids who had been in bad accidents, and kids with illnesses who just loved baseball. That tradition continues today.

Most recently it was outfielder and designated hitter Ruben Sierra who kept this particular Yankee tradition, and when rookie second baseman Robinson Cano made the team, Ruben took him under his wing. Together they would travel to hospitals such as the Hackensack University Medical Center in New Jersey, visiting children with all sorts of cancers. Robbie Cano was greatly affected by what he saw and by the joy his mere presence was able to bring to these seriously ill kids. He cared so much about these kids that it hurt.

As someone who has been a part of the Yankees organization for over thirty years, I have absorbed all those years of Yankee tradition. I've not only been lucky enough to experience it myself, from the Reggie Jackson era to the present, but to have heard the stories about all the greats from Ruth and Gehrig to DiMaggio, Mantle, and Maris from guys who were there and experienced it themselves. The Yankees are my great extended family, and like the Ruben Sierras and Robbie Canos of this world, all the individuals associated with the team have helped me when I was down. They have given me courage to deal with life when it throws an unhittable curveball at me.

I hope *The Boy of Steel* helps you to have courage in the face of adversity, to never give up, and to always try your hardest.

—RAY NEGRON

DEAR PARENTS,

The Boy of Steel is a very important, contemporary book for anyone who plays sports, and for basic human living. The story is about a boy named Michael, a child with cancer, who demonstrates authentic resilience and strength of character to proceed, in spite of his condition, to "get the job done" in his young life.

The Boy of Steel teaches us all about the relevance of staying open to ideas, about trusting in one another, about dealing with unnerving emotional experiences head on, about staying positive, and about being true to your core values. The book illustrates the power of care and compassion, as expressed by adults—in this case, by major league baseball players.

The book will have a positive effect on children, whether they have it read to them by a parent or other adult, or whether they can read it themselves.

I very much encourage you to read the book *with* your children, not just once but many times over. With this book as a parental guide, you will develop great opportunities to talk about many things that may be of concern and confusing to your kids, things about which they do not know how to ask. These include tough-to-address topics like: What is cancer? What's a neuroblastoma? How does chemotherapy work? Why is Michael bald? Is he going to die? Who really cares about him? *The Boy of Steel* will be a great springboard to really involve yourself in quality time with your children.

In addition, the book's story can be used by teachers and youth sports coaches to focus on how participation in baseball and other sports requires perspective—you must balance sports with school and life.

I have been a sport psychologist for twenty-five years and I am excited about the potential of *The Boy of Steel* to teach children that it's not all about hitting home runs and winning, but it's how you play the game—the game of life—that really counts.

Sincerely,

DR. CHARLIE MAHER
Professor of Psychology, Graduate School of Applied and Professional Psychology, Rutgers University
Team Sport Psychologist, Cleveland Indians and Cleveland Cavaliers

ACKNOWLEDGMENTS

This book could not have been possible without the help and guidance of the following people:

Tom Hopke, Nancy Ellis, Judith Regan, Doug Grad, Laura Seeley, Alison Stoltzfus, Anthony Colletti, Shawn Powell, Randy and Mindy Levine, Mort Fleishner, Theresa Bunger, Bob Klapisch, Toni Negron, Joey Negron, Jon-Erik Negron, Ricky Negron, Michael Windishman Jr., Michael Valdez, Joseph Kenyan, Robinson Cano, Ken Davidoff, David Jurist, Lt. Kelli Webb, Christine Mathews, Anthony Epps, Lou Melendez, MLB, Bob Unger, Chris Ruddy, Jim Madorma, Hector Pagan, the New York State Police, Carl Ferraro, Robert Narvaez, George N. Tim, the Marriott Marquis, Miguel Montas, La Carridad, Ceaser Presbott, Sy Preston, Amanda Hill, Fred Cambria, Tom Giordano, Norman Dina and Dianna Twain, Terri Jenkins, Suzyn Waldman, Todd Wilkens and family, the Winans, Boys of Springfield, Walter Levine, Joey Gian, John Hart, Sonny Hight, Jon Heymon, John Harper, Jack Curry, Bart Hernandez, Chuck Feinstein, the New York Yankees, the Alomar family, Walt "No-Neck" Williams, Mead Chasky, the late Gregory Hines, the Gooden family, Reed Bergman, the Lymphoma Foundation, the American Cancer Society, Joe Torre, Mr. and Mrs. Rudy Jaramillo, Mr. and Mrs. Ray Aguilla, Vincent Kenyon, Bob Ponce, Spalding, Regent Sports, Brian Cashman, Omar Minaya, Ron Dock, Hackensack University Medical Center, Sloan-Kettering, St. Joseph's Hospital, Turn 2 Foundation, Scott Clark, Steve Fortunato, Mark Mandrake, Mary Dromerhauser, Adolfo Carrion, the New York Board of Trade, John Campy, James Fiorentino, Mickey Freiberg, Al Goldis, Kristin Maloney, Terri Jenkins, Mary Pollino, Brian Smith, Julio Pabon, George King, Kevin Kernin, Gary Krupski, the Roberto Clemente family, Felix Millan, Ben Morelli, Frankie Valli and the Four Seasons, Gary Puckett, Bruce's Bakery, the Moffit Cancer Research Center, St. Jude's Childrens Hospital, the Mickey Mantle family, the Babe Ruth family, the Roger Maris family, the Lou Gehrig family, the Joe DiMaggio family, Jerry Romolt, the Barry Halper family, Ralph Paniagua, Father Tom Hartman, Harold Reynolds, Richard Seko, Jean Afterman, Kathy Bennett, Tony Morante, Josephine Doring, Debbie Nicolosie, Debbie Tyman, Shirley Beauchamp, Joann Nastell, Judith Wells, Diane Blanco, Jackie William, the Yomiuri Giants, Bobby Rossi, Robert Skollar, Donna Valenti, Dave Valle, Juan Vene, Josh Zaide, Andy Garcia, the late Dick Howser, Darryl Strawberry, Billy Martin Jr., Alex Rodriguez, Billy Berroa, Beto Villa, the N.Y. Latin Press Core, the Bunger Surf Shop, John Szponar, Howard Grosswirth, Reggie Jackson ("Mr. October"), Puerto Rico USA Imports, and Drs. Peter Scardino, Head of Urology, and Patrick Borgen, Chief Breast Surgeon, both at Sloan-Kettering, for the many lives you have saved.

—RAY NEGRON

A note of sincere gratitude to John Hulls. With appreciation to Jim and Kim Kennedy, Cameron Shapoorian, Ricky Negron, Joslin Perala, Dr. Nicholas Petty, Michael Fisher, Harris Goodman, and special thanks to Stephen Cole.

—LAURA SEELEY